Karen M- the bestselling a ⋯ ⋯ ⋯ e *Indie Kidd* serie ⋯ ell as other fiction for children and teenagers. She used to write for magazines *J17* and *Sugar*. Karen lives in London with her husband, small daughter and two fat cats.

Lydia Monks won the Smarties Prize for *I Wish I Were a Dog*. She has illustrated many poetry, novelty and picture books for children, including the *Girl Zone* series for Walker Books. Lydia lives in Sheffield with her husband and daughter.

For Cecily

(though she'll have to grow up a little bit before she can read this dedication!)

KMcC

First published 2006 by Walker Books Ltd
87 Vauxhall Walk, London SE11 5HJ

This edition published 2007

2 4 6 8 10 9 7 5 3 1

Text © 2006 Karen McCombie
Illustrations © 2006 Lydia Monks

The right of Karen McCombie and Lydia Monks to be identified as author and illustrator respectively of this work has been asserted by them in accordance with the Copyright, Designs and Patents Act 1988

This book has been typeset in Granjon

Printed and bound in Great Britain by
Creative Print and Design (Wales), Ebbw Vale

British Library Cataloguing in Publication Data:
a catalogue record for this book is available from the British Library

ISBN 978-1-4063-0720-7

www.walkerbooks.co.uk

Are We Having Fun Yet? (Hmm?)

Karen McCombie  Lydia Monks

Stressed fish
and bad news

I was **VERY** glad to see my step-brother Dylan.

OK. I was *quite* pleased to see Dylan, and **VERY** pleased to see he had some kind of big cake in his hand.

"We have to eat this," he said.

Yeah, like we were just going to look at it, I don't think…

"Better come in, then," I said, holding the door open for him.

Oh, boy – my friends Soph and Fee were going to be

SOOOOOO

glad they decided to come back to mine after school today.

"Indie!" I heard my step-mum Fiona call out from her car. "Can you two try my new recipe and tell me what you think?"

"Sure!!" I nodded, thinking that I was

SOOOOOO

glad to have a step-mum who cooks for a living.

"Where's she going?" I asked Dylan, as Fiona zoomed off in her car.

"Can't remember."

"When's she picking you up?"

"Don't know."

Those two answers might've made Dylan sound like he's pretty dumb, but really, he's a nine-year-old brainbox when it comes to school stuff. He's just lousy at normal everyday things, like chatting and making sense.

"Go on through to the kitchen," I told him, though he was already heading that way, holding the plate with the cake up high above his head.

He was holding it so high 'cause my dogs had gone into a sniffing frenzy. The way George, Kenneth and Dibbles were acting, you'd think Dylan was carrying a dog food pie, instead of a cake.

"It is a kind of *cake*, isn't it?" I checked with Dylan, as I walked behind him on my tiptoes and peeked at the suspiciously dark, gloopy filling.

"My mum called it a **Shoe Fly Pie**," mumbled Dylan, walking into the kitchen and handing the plate to Soph without bothering to say hello.

A **Shoe Fly Pie**? I fretted to myself. I think I'd rather eat one made of dog food...

"What's a **Shoe Fly Pie**?!" asked Soph, quickly shoving the plate towards Fee, as if she was playing a game of Pass the Smelly Parcel.

Fee **wrinkled** and **crinkled** her freckly nose in disgust, holding the plate out as far as her arms could stretch, and then a little bit more.

Dylan didn't answer Soph's question — he was too busy checking out the newest foster pets in our house. They were a tank of sickly fish that Mum had brought home from the *Paws For Thought* Animal Rescue Centre where she works.

"Hey, wait a minute – I know what this is!" Fee said suddenly, uncrinkling her nose and sounding strangely excited at the idea of eating the strange pie. "I had it when I was on holiday in America!"

"What is it, then?" I asked.

I knew Fee had been to Florida. And I knew they had alligators in Florida. Maybe the brown gloop was some kind of alligator stew.

Bleurghhhhh...

"It's pastry, with a filling that's made of sugar, molasses, and, um, more sugar!"

I frowned at Fee for a second, worried that molasses was a type of alligator.

"Molasses is like treacle," Fee explained, spotting the worried look on my face.

The worried look on my face instantly changed to a *very* happy look, I was sure. A kind of cake made out of sugar, treacle, and more sugar sounded very alright to me.

"But why's it called a **Shoe Fly Pie**?" asked Soph, looking for stray sprinklings of bluebottles or garnishes of shoelaces round the edge.

"It's '**shoo**', as in 'go away'," explained Fee. "A **Shoofly Pie** is supposed to be so sugary and yum, all the bees and bugs and flies swarm to it, and you have to shoo them away!"

"I'll get a knife," I said, while shooing my dogs away from the plate.

"What kind are these?" asked Dylan, still staring into the fish tank.

Weird. He was more interested in fish than food.

"Goldfish," I told him.

"Can we not talk about goldfish, please, and just have some pie?" pleaded Fee.

Fish were a touchy subject for Fee. Her **FIERCE** cat Garfield had eaten all the fish in her neighbour's garden pond yesterday.

He'd eaten all their frogs too. He must've been very hungry, or bored (in a bad way).

Fee's family had kept him locked in the house since then, till the neighbour calmed down. But it hadn't made Garfield calm down – Fee said he'd growled and hissed all night and clawed a big hole in the bathroom mat.

"But they don't exactly *look* like goldfish…" muttered Dylan.

He was obviously thinking about One, Two, Three, Four and Five, who lived happily and healthily in the tank in my living room, along with Brian the Angelfish.

"No, you're right – they don't look *much* like goldfish," Soph joined in, leaning over to stare at the four fish flitting around the fake seaweed in the tank.

"Their tails and fins are all pretty and lacy!"

"Um, that's 'cause they've got fin-rot," I told my friends.

Mum said fin-rot happens when fish are stressed. I don't know what had happened to make these fish so stressed; it's not like they had to worry about home-work or spots or anything.

Mum had taken them home from the rescue centre 'cause she thought it was

TOO NOISY

with all the barking going on there, and didn't want them to get even more stressed. The problem was, Mum seemed to have forgotten that we had three barky dogs of our own. *And* we had a lodger (nineteen-year-old Caitlin, my childminder) who played the didgeridoo.

very, very **LOUDLY.**

"Yuck!" squeaked Fee, crinkling up her nose. "Can we not talk about rotting fins? I want to eat pie!"

Fee was very squeamish about stuff like that. I think it was because of her **FIERCE** cat Garfield; his hobby was killing small things and hiding chewed bits of them around the house. (It made me very glad that my cat Smudge's hobby was pretending to be a furry sofa cushion.)

"Hey, Indie…" Soph said now, pointing somewhere behind the seaweed at the back of the tank. "See that fish there? Is it doing a trick?"

Soph was pointing at one particular upside-down fish.

I wasn't an expert or anything, but from my experience, I didn't think goldfish did tricks – they left that to dolphins.

And upside-down wasn't really the right way round for a goldfish to be.

"Um, I'm pretty sure it's DEAD," I said reluctantly.

AW...!

cried Soph and Dylan at the same time.

"That's it!" announced Fee. "No more talking about fish, or fin-rot, or dead things—"

Fee was probably about to tell us to shut up and eat pie, when Caitlin poked her head around the kitchen door.

"Fee? Phone for you – it's your mum."

As Fee hurried out into the hall, Soph's eyes twinkled with tricksiness.

"Hey, Indie – let's you, me and Dylan get a slice of pie, hide the rest, and pretend we've eaten it all when Fee comes back!" she giggled.

"Er, I wouldn't fool around with Fee just now," said Caitlin. "Her mum's got bad news – her cat died." **Gulp.**

Me and Soph and Dylan were so stunned and sorry for Fee that we all went quiet. Till Dylan came up with a sweet but stupid suggestion.

"Y'know, I think we should give ALL the pie to Fee," he declared.

Like I said before, Dylan is smart at lots of things and dumb at others. He didn't get that Fee would be so sad that the last thing she'd want to do was eat a *whole* pie, however sugary

and treacly

and yum it was.

But, uh-oh – how do you make someone who's *super-sad* feel better…?

Very funny
(I DON'T think)

Soph is the colour of coffee. I'm the colour of a cup of tea that's been made way too milky. Fee is the colour of milk, only paler. That's important to know, so you get an

idea of how Fee **looked** after crying all the way to her house. Put it this way, if it was me or Soph, we'd be a bit pink-eyed and soggy. But 'cause she's so whitely white skinned, poor Fee's eyes and nose looked like three raspberries on a snow-man's face.

"Can I see him, Mum? I want to give him one last cuddle…" Fee sniffled.

Mrs Dean winced.

Urgh – I got the feeling there wasn't that much of Garfield left to cuddle…

"That's not *such* a good idea, honey."

"Please, Mum!" Fee sniffled some more.

Soph and Dylan wriggled in their chairs, wondering if

we'd done the right thing, hanging around after we'd walked Fee home from mine.

"Fee," I butted in, trying to help Mrs Dean out, "my mum says it's always better to remember pets when they were alive and happy."

It was just a shame that Garfield was at his happiest when he was killing things. But saying what I said seemed to work – Fee shrugged an OK and stopped asking to see him.

Mrs Dean mouthed *"thank you"* at me. But, really, I was just glad to help my friend. After all, with Mum working at the rescue centre, I knew that a lot of the very old or very sick animals weren't going to make it. I mean, when they died, it still made me sadder than sad, but I guess I didn't get as madly, badly, raspberry-eyed sad as Fee was feeling right now.

"I bet Mr Petropoulos is *really* pleased," Fee mumbled darkly.

"Now that's not fair, Fee – I'm *sure* Mr Petropoulos was very upset."

I don't think what Mrs Dean said was true. Yes, so Fee's neighbour had gone to the trouble of picking Garfield up and letting Mrs Dean know what had happened. But since Garfield had eaten everything that lived in and around his pond, Mr Petropoulos probably *wasn't* going to cry himself to sleep tonight.

So how *had* BIG, growly, scary old Garfield died?

It had to be something *very* dramatic.

1. Had he daringly scrambled up (and fallen out of) the highest of high trees?

2. Had he bravely started (and lost) a fight with the meanest and toughest dog in the neighbourhood?

3. Had he been wrestling (and got swallowed by) a stray boa constrictor that had escaped from the zoo.

Nope.

Garfield the **FIERCE** had been **squished** by a delivery van.

If he had to get run over, being squished by a huge juggernaut or a Formula One racing car might've been a cool way to go.

Instead, he'd snuck out of the open loo window in Fee's house, hurtled across the garden, and **z o o m e d** straight into the path of a delivery van that was tootling along at the speed of a snail with a walking stick.

So *not* cool.

(I bet Mr Petropoulos was writing a Thank You letter to the van driver right now, on behalf of his ex-frogs and fish.)

sniffle sniffle

"LISTEN," said Fee's mum, giving Fee's shoulders a comforting squeeze, "I *know* it feels bad right now, but it won't feel *so awful* in time…"

Fee instantly dropped her gaze to the floor and starting sobbing. From this angle, all you could see was a tumbling swirl of red curls bouncing up and down.

I saw Soph grab a tissue out of a nearby box and pass it through the wavy curtain of hair, in the vague direction of Fee's nose.

Dylan, I noticed, was frowning.

I knew that frown – it meant his clever-clogs brain was **whirring** madly, thinking hard. I guessed what was up: I'd said something helpful to Fee, Soph had just done something helpful for Fee, and now he was trying to figure out how he could be helpful to our friend too.

Ping!!

The frown vanished and Dylan's eye-brows shot up. He'd thought of something!

"What's furry and dizzy?" he asked.

No one answered him ...

A because we didn't know the answer,

AND

B because we didn't know *what* he was on about.

"A cat on a roundabout!" Dylan burst out. "What's furry and wobbles?"

Huh?! What was Dylan up to?

"A cat on top of a washing machine!

What's furry and loud?"

Dylan didn't seem a bit put-off that no one was answering him, or that me, Soph and Mrs Dean were all staring at him like he'd gone bananas.

"A cat doing karaoke! What's furry and goes WHEE! SPLAT! OOPS!?"

And then I got it! Not the jokes so much, but the fact that Dylan was doing his best to cheer Fee up by making her laugh. What a *brilliant* idea! Why didn't I think of that?

"A cat falling off of its skateboard. What's furry and giggles?"

I was just about to jump in with an answer when Fee lifted her head, sending curls spiralling.

She stared at Dylan with her watery, raspberry eyes and snapped, "How CAN you tell jokes at a time like this?" before **PARPING** her raspberry nose on the tissue that Soph had handed to her.

Er, what was I saying about the joke thing being an EXCELLENT idea?

I wanted to cheer Fee up, but it didn't look like making her laugh was going to work.

What could me, Dylan and Soph try next?

I'd have to have a good think about that, and come up with a better **Cheer Up Fee** Plan.

(And I'd have to wait till we were safely outside to ask Dylan if the answer to "What's furry and giggles?" was "A cat that's just heard a really good joke...")

3

Comfort cookies

The next morning was Saturday, and for our next try at cheering up Fee, I'd made cookies.

Well, not just me;
I had a little help to make them *extra-specially good* cookies.

In case you're wondering, the help didn't come from Caitlin (who can burn soup), or my mum (who was busy working at the rescue centre).

Actually, even if she'd been at home, Mum wouldn't have been able to help much. My dad once said that her cooking was as good as my driving. I was five at the time, so I guess that was his way of saying she was rubbish near a cooker.

He's right; I don't think Mum knows what an oven's for. She's got some packets of dried rabbit food and a stack of unused, weird-shaped jelly moulds stored in ours just now.

I'm not being *mean* about my mum when I say that. Mum is very helpful at other things, like showing you how to bottle-feed baby mice and give antibiotics to sick goldfish. But she's not much use when you want to make chocolate chip cookies.

Which is where Fiona came in. Maybe one of the reasons why Dad is happy to be married to Fiona is that she spends all day, every day trying out new recipes for her cookery column in the local paper.

And, yes, Fiona was the someone who'd been very helpful to me – in a cooking cookies way – this morning.

Yep, I know I'd pooh-poohed Dylan's foodie idea, the one about giving Fee the entire **Shoofly Pie** to eat the second we heard about Garfield. But it had now been *nineteen and three quarter* hours since the bad news, so I thought Fee might be up for a bit of comfort eating.

Or at least comfort nibbling.

"Mmm ... they smell great. Can I have one?" asked Soph, lifting the corner of the plastic box and drooling.

Me, Soph, and the cookies were
sitting on a picnic blanket in the park.
Dylan and my three dogs were lolloping
around somewhere close by.

"ABSOLUTELY NOT!"
I scolded Soph. "They're a present for Fee,
to cheer her up!"

"But she can't eat *all* of them!" Soph
practically whimpered.

"Yeah, I know," I said, "but we have to
wait for her to offer us one."

I didn't dare tell Soph that me and Dylan had *already* eaten two each as soon as they came out of the oven (all hot and melty – mmm!), or that we'd taken turns eating chocolate chip cookie gloop straight from the bowl (drool).

If I told Soph that, she'd **moan, moan, moan** that it wasn't fair, and **pester, pester, pester** me till she got one. Or more likely two, to catch up with us.

Then I'd HAVE to have another one. *Why?* Because it's the law, when it comes to cookies.

And Dylan would have another one. *(Of course.)*

And the dogs would all want a bit of one.

And all that would be left in the box would be one and a half cookies and some chocolate crumbs. Which would still taste good, but wouldn't look like much of a present.

"Fee was *pretty* miserable yesterday – maybe she isn't going to come," Soph suggested.

She had a sympathetic look on her face, but I couldn't help wondering if Soph sort of slightly hoped Fee wasn't going to show

up, from a cookie point of view…
"Hey!
Here comes Fee now!"

Dylan panted, thundering up to us with three barking dogs in hot pursuit.

Uh-oh…

It might have been *nineteen and three quarter* hours since our friend had heard the bad news about her cat, but she still looked gutted.

In fact, I'd never seen *anyone* ride a bike so sadly.

If she cycled any more slowly the bike would fall over.

"Mmmmm..." Fee mumbled, *flopping* off, *flinging* her bike on its side on the grass, and *flooping* herself miserably onto the blanket beside us.

Fee must've smelled too sad for Kenneth and George; after a quick, wary sniff, they both scuttled off to investigate a nearby tree trunk.

But Dibbles, my dog of very little brain, was more sensitive, and thunked his big, cannonball head down on Fee's lap.

"How are you feeling today?" I asked her.

"Hnufffinummm..."

Fee mumbled some more

46

and shrugged vaguely.

She didn't look so much like a raspberry-eyed snowman today, but you could tell by the puffiness of her face that she'd been doing plenty more crying in the last *nineteen and three quarter* hours.

"What's wrong with your arms?" Dylan suddenly asked.

"And what's happened to your chest?!" Soph added.

Huh?

For a second, I thought that something like "Are you OK?" would have been a better question for Dylan and Soph to have come out with.

And then I spotted the, er, spots.

"What *is* that?" I joined in, bending over for a closer look at the tiny pink bumps dotted across her white skin.

"Garfield's blankie…" Fee mumbled, lifting her T-shirt up a bit to show off a dotty tummy too. "I got bitten."

"By a blankie?!" asked Dylan, blinking and bewildered.

"By fleas on it, right?" I jumped in.

I know lots of interesting (and interestingly yucky) stuff about animals, thanks to my mum. Like I know that cat fleas aren't remotely interested in biting humans while there's a cat in the house to snack on. But the minute the cat's gone, fleas tend to heave a sigh and decide that humans will have to do…

"Yep, fleas," nodded Fee, dropping her T-shirt and **scratch-scratch-**

scratching her itchily spotty arms.

"But how come the fleas hopped all the way from the blankie in Garfield's basket onto you?" asked Soph.

"'Cause I took it out of the basket and cuddled it in bed all last night, just to be *close* to Garfield…"

Just to be close to Garfield's fleas, more like.

Poor Fee; she'd lost a cat, and ended up with a rash that looked like a bad case of chickenpox.

"Hey, have these. They're chocolate chip – I made them for you this morning," I said, quickly offering her the comfort cookies.

"No, thanks," moaned Fee. "I haven't been able to eat since … you know. Even just looking at toast this morning made me feel sick."

"That's so sad!" Soph said kindly.

With one hand, she patted Fee comfortingly on the shoulder.

With both eyes, she gazed *longingly* at Fee's cookies.

"Can I have one, then?" Dylan asked straight out, subtle as a slab of concrete.

Fee nodded and shrugged – and Soph and Dylan instantly dived in and grabbed a cookie each.

Good grief... how greedy, I thought.

And then straight away, I thought something else: the speed Dylan and Soph are eating, there really will only be crumbs left in the box soon!

Feeling bad(ish), I grabbed a comfort cookie and started nibbling too.

Well, I needed energy to help me come up with a brand new **Cheer Up Fee** Plan...

The not-a-happy-bunny poem

Fee hung out with us in the park for *exactly* eight minutes – just long enough for me, Soph and Dylan to finish her comfort cookies, and for her to go demented with **itching** from the flea bites.

"Don't go!" I mumbled, through a mouthful of cookie. "We 'aven't 'ad a chance to talk prop'ly!"

(And nope, I certainly wasn't talking

properly with all that cookie crammed in my mouth.)

"Got to," Fee said, slipping her phone in her pocket and getting ready to cycle away and meet her mum. "The chemist closes at midday and I need to get something for the **itching**."

"Wanna meet tomorrow?" I suggested, gulping hard and feeling guilty for spending the last couple of minutes eating and checking out flea bites, and not really making Fee feel any better.

"OK, where?"

A rush of sugar to the brain got me thinking of a brand, new **Cheer Up Fee** Plan at last.

"The shopping centre – in the café, at about 11 o'clock?"

"Cool," Fee shrugged sadly, then cycled off, at a sloth's pace.

"Wow, she is **S O O O O O O** miserable," said Soph, watching as Fee frantically scratched some flea bites, wobbled

and nearly crashed into a holly bush.

"Wow, Dibbles's tongue feels sooo weird and rough!" said Dylan, watching as Dibbles licked all the cookie crumbs off his knees.

I shot a *can't-you-think-about-Fee?* glare his way, but Dylan was too busy trying to grab Dibbles's tongue for a closer look to notice.

Anyway, that was *then*,
and this was *now*.

What I mean is, that was yesterday (Saturday), and now it was today (Sunday), and me, Soph and Dylan were in the shopping centre, surrounded by people walking in s l o o o o w w w w motion.

(What's all that about? s l o o o o w w w w -motion shopping on a Sunday? Check it out: on Monday, Tuesday, Wednesday, Thursday, Friday and Saturday, most people trot around the shops pretty speedily. Then it gets to Sunday and

everyone

s l o o o o w w w w s s s s
r i i i g g h h h h t t t
d o o o o w w w w n n n n , '

as if their shopping batteries have run out.)

"That is the *cutest* thing. Fee is going to love it," Soph cooed into the plastic bag I was carrying.

We'd just been in the toy shop, spending all our pocket money on a **Cheer Up Fee** present. This time the present wasn't edible, it was huggable.

"I still liked the robot-that-turned-into-

a-pirate-ship better," said Dylan, uselessly.

I didn't bother answering. I think even a moth or a stick would have the sense to know that when someone is badly missing their dead cat, a robot-that-turns-into-a-pirate-ship isn't really going to get them tap-dancing with happiness.

Luckily for Fee, the present we had bought her was a soft toy. Not *any old* soft toy, though. Yesterday in the park, what had **POW-ed** into my head was the fact that one of Fee's favourite DVDs was "Garfield – The Movie" (she named her own cat after the grouchy puss in that film).

After that **POW!**, I realized in a split-second that Fee would love a Garfield toy. It was fat, furry and cute, and would be nicer to cuddle in bed than a blankie full of hungry fleas.

So that's why I suggested meeting up in the shopping centre – to give me, Soph and Dylan the chance to go to the toy shop, and buy a robot-that-turns-into-a-pirate-ship (only joking).

"Look, Fee's there already!" said Soph, pointing in the direction of a table by the window.

Normally, Fee would be sitting with a carton of apple juice, a blueberry muffin and a BIG smile for us by now.

Today, there was nothing much on the table except a packet of tissues (her tummy was still on strike, it looked like). And instead of smiling our way, her ringletty head was bent down as she scribbled into her diary.

"Hey! Hi, Fee!" I said, as we reached the table.

(I don't know about super-human powers like turning invisible or being a human spider; I suddenly just wished I could read words upside-down. That'd be cool. And, er, it would mean I could peek at what Fee had been writing without looking v. v. rude.)

"Hi," muttered Fee, glancing up at as all with big, squidgy dollops of tears threatening to spill down her cheeks.

"Oh, Fee! Are you all gloomy again?"

asked Soph, slipping into the seat next to her and putting her arm around Fee's shoulders.

Dylan moved behind Soph and leant over. Aw, he was going to hug Fee too!

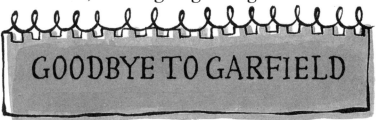

GOODBYE TO GARFIELD

he read out loud.

"Dylan!" I yelped, realizing what he was actually doing. "You don't read people's diaries! They're private!"

"It's OK," said Fee, dabbing her eyes with a scrunched-up, slighty snotty-looking tissue. "It's a poem I've written for—"

Fee couldn't quite get her pusscat's name out – it seemed to get stuck behind the sadness in her throat.

"Read it out, Dylan!" said Soph, giving him a nod to get on with it.

GOODBYE TO GARFIELD
Oh, Garfield, Garfield, I am so blue...

Uh-oh. Fee wasn't exactly a happy bunny at the moment, and already this sounded like a very not-a-happy-bunny poem.

Our house is so empty without you...

Yeah, empty of half-chewed goldfish and frogs, I thought.

I miss **stroking** your orange fur for hours...

Hissss

WHAT? Everytime Fee tried to stroke him Garfield hissed at her.

And I miss hearing that **sweet** miaow of yours...

Y'know, sadness must have fuzzed up the memory part of Fee's brain. Garfield's miaow wasn't sweet; it sounded like someone playing a violin with a cheese grater.

> Oh, Garfield, Garfield, my darling kitten...

"That's as far as I've got," sniffled Fee. "I couldn't think what to rhyme with 'kitten'."

I could see her problem.

The only word that popped into my head was "mitten", and even with a fuzzed-up mind, I didn't know how Fee could write something cute about Garfield and mittens.

Only that he might have used one to hide a dead frog in.

"Um, it's a *lovely* poem, Fee," I lied, crossing the fingers of one hand behind my back. "Here – we've got something for you. We clubbed together to get it…"

With my other hand, I passed her the bag with the toy in it.

For a second, Fee almost had a tiny flicker of a glimmer of a smile showing … until she opened up the bag and saw the cheekily grinning fat face of Garfield the soft toy beaming up at her.

"It's a—

a—

a – *lovely* present," she said sadly, lying as much to us as I had to her a second ago.

65

"But?"

The "but?" came from Dylan. Like I say, he can be smart when he wants to, and he knew there was an unspoken "but" floating just inside Fee's mouth.

"But it's the *wrong* Garfield, isn't it?" Fee blurted out. "It just reminds me that it's not him."

Standing behind her, Soph blinked all panic-striken at me. And Dylan, well, Dylan was mouthing, "Told you so!"

I frowned and mouthed a "Huh?!" back at him.

Instantly he held his arms out, clenched his teeth together and looked nuts. Just as instantly, he linked his fingers together and rocked them, then slapped a hand over one

eye and hopped a bit.

OK, I got it, this mad mime of Dylan's.

I rolled my eyes and sighed silently. Nope – the robot-that-turned-into-a-pirate-ship would not have been a better **Cheer Up Fee** Plan.

But what *was*?

It was time to …

A take Garfield the toy cat back to the shop for a refund,

and

B get thinking of a new **Cheer Up Fee** Plan – before Fee wrote any more terrible poems…

The HORRIBLY truthful poem

Monday morning, 9.02 a.m., and I was nearly nodding off at my school desk – all because I'd been tossing and turning all night, trying to think of a new **Cheer Up Fee** Plan.

I should've just chilled-out and had a good sleep, 'cause even with all that tossing and turning, I'd come up with minus-zero ideas.

And I'd woken Dibbles up with all the tossing and turning. So he started tossing and turning at the bottom of my bed, and

then it felt a bit like I was trying to go to sleep on a trampoline.

Anyway, back to Monday morning.

(Y a a a w w w n n n ...)

ON THE UPSIDE:
Fee's red, itchy spots were a lot better (thanks to the medicine she'd been taking the last couple of days).

ON THE DOWNSIDE:
she looked as if she was going to a fancy dress party as a stick of liquorice (thanks to the fact that she was dressed ALL in black).

"SOPHIE DEAN!"

Miss Levy, our teacher called out, taking Monday morning register.

Fee mumbled miserably.

Miss Levy instantly looked up.

Mumbling "Here Miss Levy…" wasn't Fee's style. Fee was always bright and chirpy and all.

"Are you alright, Sophie?" our teacher asked.

Fee nodded, and glanced down at

the desk.

Hmm. Wasn't she going to tell Miss Levy about Garfield?

Maybe not. Maybe Fee was scared she'd start sniffling and snuffling in front of the whole class.

I noticed Miss Levy's eyes scanning Fee.

From her expression, I knew she could tell that Fee wasn't alright.

It wasn't just 'cause Fee was clutching a box of man-size tissues to her chest. (I think all the shops for miles around had run out of pocket-size packs, 'cause of Fee's mammoth eye-dabbing and nose-blowing sessions.)

It was also
because Miss Levy
was checking
out what Fee
was wearing.
And what she was
wearing wasn't what
Fee *normally* wore.
Y'see, Fee loves purple
(and mauve and lavender and
plum…). In fact, she mostly
always wears something pur-
ple-ish, 'most every single day.
But today, Fee was wearing a
black T-shirt, black trousers
and black shoes – with a
black hairband in her red,
curly-wurly hair too.

"Black's the colour of *mourning*," she'd told me and Soph in the playground earlier.

"What does *'mourning'* mean again?" Soph had asked, looking at our stick-of-liquorice friend.

Fee knew

LOTS

of big words (she's good at that sort of thing), but I knew this one too, and thought maybe it would be easier if I explained to Soph.

"It's like when people die," I'd begun.

"Or cats," Fee'd added quickly.

"Or cats," I'd corrected myself. "Anyway, mourning is the time when everyone feels a bit sad for whoever – or whatever's – died, and they dress in black to show how *sad* they are."

Anyway, right now, Miss Levy was checking out the general *miserableness* of Fee, and looked as if she was just about to quiz her some more ... and then she stopped, and got on to the next name on the register.

I had a feeling Miss Levy thought it would be better to talk to Fee on her own later.

Or better still ... maybe it would be better still if I explained to Miss Levy what had happened!

I mean, if I (quietly) told our teacher what was going on, it would mean that ...

A Miss Levy would understand why Fee was dressed as a stick of liquorice,

and

B poor, in-mourning, liquorice-girl Fee wouldn't have to say stuff and get upset again.

YEP, the more I thought about it, the more I decided that it was a good sort of **Cheer Up Fee** Plan and definitely a nice thing to do.

And as I thought
  (and thought),
        I began to doodle
        (and doodle) in my workbook.
Think, THINK, doodle, DOODLE.
Think, THINK, doodle, DOO—

INDIE! That was Soph *hissing* my name, nudging me with her sharp elbow and making my last doodly word squiggle a bit.

"What?" I frowned at her, just before I heard Miss Levy say, "INDIA KIDD! Are you on another planet? Or will I have to say your name another *three* times before you answer?"

Uh-oh.

I'd been so busy and doodly for the last couple of minutes that I hadn't heard Miss Levy call out my name those

    one,

        two,

            three

                times.

And I hadn't noticed her wander away from her big teacher desk and come and stand right in front of mine.

"What's been taking up your attention, Indie?" she asked, scooping my doodled-on workbook before I could blink.

"It's … uh … nothing."

"*Nothing*, eh?" Miss Levy frowned down at me. "Well, this *nothing* of yours looks like a poem to me. Let's see what this is about, since it stopped you from recognizing your own name…"

Aaarghhhhhhhhh!!!

went a tiny voice in my head, as I realized what exactly I'd been doodling.

But it was *too late*.

Miss Levy had already picked up my workbook and started reading out of it. Reading out a horribly truthful poem about Garfield. The sort of horribly truthful poem that wasn't ever meant to be seen or heard by Fee.

Oh, *please, please, please,* let a large hole open up in the ground underneath me, or a large herd of rampaging badgers run over me and squidge me to death.

Anything instead of have Fee stare so hard at me right now, as she listened to every word Miss Levy read from my book.

Oh, Garfield, Garfield,
you were so fierce,
There were so MANY things
that you liked to pierce.
skin, frogs, goldfish and mice,
To humans and animals you
weren't very nice.

Urgh.

If there was one thing guaranteed not to cheer Fee up, it was a horribly truthful poem like that.

"Indie!
　　How could you!!"

Fee gasped, as she sniffled into a man-size tissue from her box.

OK. Right now I needed an

extra, extra-special,
super-dooper,
jump-up-and-down,
wow-whee

of an idea to cheer Fee up, before she decided to dump me as a best friend for ever...

Saying sorry (a lot)

OK.

So making your best friend *more miserable than ever* is the opposite of trying to cheer her up.

I'd really goofed with that stupid, horribly truthful poem.

I'd tried saying sorry (a lot). And I'd even pointed out some long-ago scratchmarks that still showed on Soph's arm to remind Fee that Garfield really used to be a teensy bit mean at times.

But all day Monday and all day Tuesday, Fee had refused to speak to me, talking through Soph any time she needed to communicate in class.

"Soph, can you ask Indie to pass me the glitter glue?" *[Fee]*

"Fee – here you go!" *[Me]*

[Silence from Fee, who ignores the hand – and the glitter glue – I'm holding out.]

"Um, here's the glitter glue from Indie." *[Soph, taking it out of my hand and passing it it on.]*

Like I say, it went on like that for
two
whole
days.

I was *desperate* to work out how I could make up with Fee AND still cheer her up, like a good friend should.

At home on Tuesday lunchtime, Caitlin came up with an idea.

"I got this DVD out the library yester-day," she told me. "It's really silly and funny. Why don't you ask Fee and your other friends around to watch it after school today? If you get Fee laughing, maybe she'll forget to be sad about her cat – or be so mad at you…"

It seemed like a very good idea. Especially to me, who had no ideas at all, not even bad ones.

The only problem was that it's quite hard to ask someone to come watch a movie at your house when they're not speaking to you.

"Fee – do you and Soph want to come to mine after school? It's just that Caitlin says we can watch this *really brilliant* movie she's got out of the library."

(Silence.)

"Um, Fee…" Soph began to repeat, "Indie wants to know—"

"Tell Indie OK," Fee had butted in, still not talking directly to me.

Phew.

She wasn't exactly speaking to me again, but agreeing to come to mine was as close as I could expect to an "I forgive you".

I was determined that we'd have a brilliant time that would be silly and funny (thanks to Caitlin's DVD) and end up with us all being friends again (I hope, hope, hoped against hope).

So now it was 3.35 p.m., and we were sprawled in my living room: Fee on the whole of the sofa (she deserved it); Soph on the armchair (sharing it with Smudge my cat); and me on the floor, with George, Kenneth and Dibbles padding about, trying to decide where *exactly* on the mat to flop down and cuddle up.

Dylan – who I'd texted at his school this afternoon – was in the kitchen, getting a bowl for the chilli popcorn my step-mum Fiona wanted us to try out for her.

Fee *still* wasn't really talking to me, but I thought a few giggles into this movie and everything would be back to normal.

Fingers crossed.

"What did you say this film was about, again, Indie?" Soph asked, as we sat through the trailers.

"Um, some students at a High School in America, getting up to dumb stuff," I said vaguely. (I had no idea *what* dumb stuff they got up to – they could be bungee-jumping with their grannies or holding **knit-your-own-toothbrush** competitions. I'd been too busy being hopeful to ask Caitlin for any details.)

Right then, Dylan came **s p e e d i n g** into the room, rammed the bowl of chilli pop-corn under my nose – and dropped a note into my lap!

I was just about to read it aloud when I saw in capital letters at the top of the note:

DO NOT READ ALOUD!

After the disaster of Miss Levy reading my horribly truthful poem out in class yesterday, I thought it would better to read this secret note as quietly as possible.

And the quietest place I knew was in my head.

Another sick goldfish just died - **don't** say in front of Fee in case it makes her cry **AGAIN.**

That was smart thinking.

Fee had cried so much in the last five days that I was starting to worry about her getting dehydrated and turning into a girl-sized version of a prune.

"Um, I'll just go get some drinks," I said, standing up and scurrying towards the kitchen.

"D'you need a hand?" asked Fee, talking directly to me for the first time in 48 hours.

NO!

I barked, then realized I should probably have tried to sound more warm and friendly.

Fee frowned, wondering why I was being so snappy. But obviously, I *didn't* exactly want her to follow me into the kitchen if there was nothing but sad, bad news going on there.

"I'll get us all more juice – that chilli popcorn is *really* hot!" I fibbed, waving at my mouth to pretend to cool it down. "Just start the movie without me – I'll catch up!"

Before I scooted through the living room door, I glanced at One, Two, Three, Four, Five, and Brian, pootling around in their tank, with no idea of the tragic fishy

event that had just happened.

Or the fact that Caitlin was just about to dump the dead goldfish in the bin like a used teabag.

"NO!" I yelled in a tiny whisper, just as Caitlin stood poised with her foot on the pedal.

I quickly stood myself in-between the bin and the tank on the worktop, so that the last two lacy-edged goldfish didn't see what had so nearly happened.

(Not that they seemed that bothered

that their buddy had just flapped his fins for the last time. They were both too busy nibbling food floating on the surface of the water.)

"But … but, er, *what else* am I supposed to do with it?" Caitlin asked, with a helpless look on her face.

"Well, bury it in the garden, next to the other one, of course!" I explained, thinking that Mum had promised to pick up a pretty plant to stick on the spot (better tell her to make it two pretty plants now).

I heard Soph's voice drift

through from the living room.

"Coming!" I yelled back, hurriedly looking under the sink for something to put DEAD GOLDFISH NO. 2 into.

"Oh, now that I *remember*, there was this ONE THING I was going to mention about that film," said Caitlin, as she softly plopped the fish into the supermarket carrier bag I was now holding out to her.

"Oh, yeah?" I mumbled, tying a knot in the top of the bag, and panicking where to

stash it till I could deal with it later.

"It is *really, really* funny, but right at the beginning, there's this stupid bit where a couple of lads in a car run over a cat. I mean they don't really – they only *pretend* to do it as a bad-taste joke to scare their girlfriends, but—"

WAAAHHHHHH!!

Through in the living room, Fee didn't seem to appreciate the bad-taste joke one little, tiny bit.

And it didn't seem like this was a great **Cheer Up Fee** Plan after all.

Better start working on **Cheer Up** Plan No. 6...

The brand-new, very, VERY good plan

"What am I going to do …

what am I going to do …

what am I going to do…?"

That could've been me, fretting about **Cheer Up Fee** Plan No. 6 – but it wasn't.

The person doing the fretting was my mum, and she was fretting over the fish tank in the kitchen.

"Are those two **alright?**" I asked her, as I cleared up the glasses and the empty chilli popcorn bowl.

(Technically, me, Fee, Soph and Dylan should still have been watching the *"funny"* DVD Caitlin had lent us. But once Fee got upset and went home, no one else was much in the mood to watch a movie and left too. Except for me, of course. I couldn't leave since I lived here.)

"This one's looking better, but this one…"

Mum trailed off, and I squinted at the goldfish to see what she was on about.

Sure enough, one goldfish was looking a little more orange-y and less

lacy than it did a few days ago. And the other fish … well, it was more a greyfish than a goldfish, which wasn't a good sign.

"We'll just have to keep going with the antibiotics and hope for the best, eh, Indie?"

"Fingers crossed," I nodded up at Mum.

When she was young, Mum used to be a model and wear fancy clothes and smell of perfume.

Now she's the boss of the Rescue Centre, lives in old trousers and smells of hamster bedding. But she's *still* a gorgeous mum, and I LOVE spending time with her like this, standing shoulder-to-shoulder, just talking about whatever.

"Anyway, is everything alright with you, Indie?" Mum asked, wrapping her arm around my waist.

(Having Mum wrap her arm around my waist is even better than standing shoulder-to-shoulder with her.)

"Kind of," I shrugged. "But Fee's still really down-in-the-dumps. And every time me, Soph and Dylan try to cheer her up, we manage to make her more miserable…"

"Sorry, Indie – I haven't been asking enough about all that," Mum apologized to me. "Things have been so hectic with work that my head's a bit full-up and fuzzy with it all."

What was new?

Ever since she went to work at the Rescue Centre, Mum's head's been full-up and fuzzy with animal stuff.

And she'd already told me that this week was specially busy 'cause of the sick fish, *and* trying to find homes for

a shy snake,

a zillion cats,

a *very* lazy pot-bellied pig

AND

a nervous old dog that weed itself every time visitors said hello to it.

(No wonder Mum's head was a bit full-up and fuzzy.)

"That's OK," I forgave Mum. "But I *wish* I could think of something to cheer up Fee."

"Remind me, what have you tried already?" asked Mum.

Well…

1. Dylan tried telling Fee jokes, but that just made her mad.

2. *Then* I tried giving her chocolate cookies, but she felt too sick to eat.

3. *Then* we all bought her a Garfield toy, but that made her miss the real Garfield even more.

4. *Then* I thought I'd be nice and tell Miss Levy about Garfield, so Fee wouldn't have to, but Miss Levy read out my NOT-NICE poem about

Garfield and Fee got angry with me.

"Oops," mumbled Mum.

I didn't *need* to tell Mum about Fee crying over the intro to Caitlin's film, 'cause she came home from work just as Fee's dad arrived to take her (and Soph and Dylan) home.

"Can you think of *anything* that would cheer Fee up, Mum?" I asked.

Mum frowned a bit, like she was thinking very, very, very hard.

That went on for quite a while, which made me hope there was a very, very, very good idea coming at the end of all that frowning.

"Indie…" Mum began. "My brain is so full-up and fuzzy that I haven't got a clue. Sorry! But how about we go bury the goldfish that died today, and I promise I'll keep on thinking my hardest?"

And so Mum and me headed for the garden – clutching the supermarket plastic bag – and gave a quick knock on Caitlin's bedroom door, so she could join us in the funeral ceremony.

'Cause she was feeling guilty for nearly chucking the dead goldfish in the bin, Caitlin took her didgeridoo out into the garden and played a lovely, sad tune on it ✪.

(✪ Er, even happy tunes sound sad on a didgeridoo. It's just that sort of sad-sounding instrument.)

As Caitlin **rumble-bumbled** her sad tune, and Mum buried the goldfish beside his old fishy friend – just left of the holly bush our cat Smudge liked to poo under – I had it.

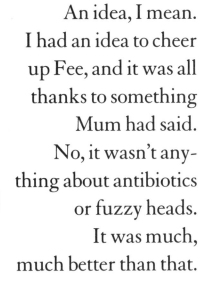

An idea, I mean. I had an idea to cheer up Fee, and it was all thanks to something Mum had said. No, it wasn't anything about antibiotics or fuzzy heads. It was much, much better than that. In fact, it was a brand-new, very, VERY good plan, and would make Fee very, VERY happy indeed. Maybe…

The Magical Mystery Tour

Cheer Up Fee Plan No. 6 was amazing.

I mean, it wasn't just good, or very good, it was

AMAZING!!

And it hadn't come a second too late. Fee was in *desperate* need of cheering up. Me, Soph and Dylan saw that as soon as we walked into her room on Thursday afternoon after school, and checked out the shrine she'd made on her chest of drawers.

Beside a big, framed photo of Garfield were …

☞ a vase of flowers
☞ Garfield's collar
☞ Garfield's food bowl
☞ Garfield's water bowl
☞ Garfield's favourite (very chewed) catnip mouse.

All that was missing was Garfield's litter tray and a half-dead frog (thank goodness).

But we'd left the smell of flowers and sadness behind and were now all outdoors, strolling slowly and carefully along the pavement. (You'll understand why in a second.)

"Wow – this is going to be so much fun!" I told Soph and Dylan, and especially Fee.

Soph and Dylan grinned back at me.

Fee looked nervous, but that was probably because she was scared of tripping, since she couldn't see where she was going with the blindfold on and everything.

Let me explain…

Cheer Up Fee Plan No. 6 was a

Magical Mystery Tour.

And the Magical Mystery Tour led from Fee's House to the *Paws For Thought* Rescue Centre.

Once we were there, we'd whip off the blindfold and Fee would be surrounded by heaps of miaowing, mewing, fluffy kitties, and she'd fall in love with one of them and want to have it for her very, very own.

How could she resist?

So that was my amazing **Cheer Up Fee** Plan – but it had been quite hard to organize.

FIRST, I'd got the idea from Mum, who'd mentioned all the *zillions* of cats she had to try and find new homes for. (Well, a shy snake or a pot-bellied pig or whatever would hardly take the place of Garfield.)

SECOND, I'd had to get my mum to phone Fee's mum, to check if she thought the **Cheer Up Fee** Plan was a good one. (*Phew* – she did.)

THIRD, I'd had to find a blindfold.

(Caitlin lent me a dark red silk scarf.)

FOURTH, me, Soph and Dylan had had to convince Fee that our "game" was going to be a good one.

But at last, along with Mrs Dean, we'd managed to persuade Fee to join in with our game.

After ten minutes of leading her bumbling and complaining from her house, we were finally there.

"Hello!" I said, and waved at Rose, the receptionist at the Rescue Centre, who was in on our secret plan.

Rose buzzed a buzzer and sprang open the door that led through to the animal buildings.

"Where are we?" asked Fee, her ears tuning into all the barking, miaowing, oinking and clucking going on.

"The moon," I joked, hurrying towards the cat block.

Fee wasn't dumb (in fact she was pretty smart), so it would only take a nano-second for her to work out that we were either at ...

A the local petting zoo at the park,
or
B the Rescue Centre.

"Indie, when can I take this scarf—"

Just as Fee was about to say the word "off?", I tugged at the bow at the back of her head and the red silk slipped away.

"Oh!" murmured Fee, her green eyes blinking at the sea of small, purry, furry faces in cages.
Dylan smiled at me.
I smiled at Soph.
Soph smiled at Dylan.

purrrrr purrrr

We all smiled at each other.

Yep, Plan No. 6 was going to work totally brilliantly, we were sure of it!

"*Oh!*" Fee murmured again, walking over to the nearest cage.

"Told you this was going to be fun!" I whispered to Dylan and Soph.

"*Cats!!*" Fee murmured yet again, sounding a bit surprised, confused and happy all at once.

"That's right!" my mum's voice drifted in the door just behind us. "Feel free to wander round and meet

them all!"

"They're so **cuuuuuttteee!!**"
Fee cooed, opening a door
and sticking her hand into
a cage of kittens and getting every finger rubbed
against and nuzzled.

"And all of them looking for
lovely new homes,' Mum
continued, throwing me a wink.

Please,
    oh, please,
        oh, PLEASE

let Fee find a new cat and be happy! I said
to myself, crossing my fingers so tight
behind my back that they were probably
turning blue.

It's just that I *missed* the old, fun Fee.

I *missed* her getting jokes.

I *missed* drooling over cookies with her.

I *missed* chatting about silly stuff and nonsense together.

I *missed* seeing her wearing shades of lilac and lavender and mauve.

If she could just get a cat and get happy, then *everything* would be back to normal.

"Aw, this one's **cute** too! *And* this one! *And* this one!"

Fee sighed, hurrying along the cages and wiggling her fingers through the mesh towards fat cats, skinny cats, glamour cats and scruffy cats.

"So which one are you going to take?" Soph burst out excitedly.

Fee stopped dead, right beside the cage of a BIG, white and black cat with a mean look and one fang glinting.

The happy smile on Fee's face had slithered away.

Uh-oh.

"What d'you *mean*, which one am I going to TAKE?" she said, her fingers clutching tightly onto the wire mesh.

"Well, which one's going to be your *new* cat?" Soph asked brightly, somehow not really realizing that Fee had gone gloomy again.

"But –

but –

I don't want a *new* cat!" Fee mumbled, with her bottom lip wibble-wobbling.

"It won't be G– G–Garfield, will it?"

Mum immediately spotted that Fee needed a mumsy moment, and hurried over, arms outstretched, just as Fee started blubbing.

At that second, the white and black, mean-looking, one-fanged cat decided to sink its one fang into Fee's hand.

Owwwwwwwwww!!

Fee yowled.

As Fee yowled and cried, and cried and yowled, Dylan shot me a panicked look.

"Indie … are we having fun yet?" he asked me.

"Hmm?" I hmmed back, watching my mum hug Fee.

It was easier to go "hmm?" than admit to Dylan that no – we definitely weren't having fun…

9

One last plan...

"Let's get that seen to," said Mum, hurrying a tearful Fee and her bitten finger towards the door.

As it swung closed behind them, me, Soph and Dylan stood in silence.

Well, silence-*ish*.

Maybe we weren't doing any talking, but there was plenty of **mewing** and **purring** going on in the background.

"Do they make very small muzzles for cats?" Dylan finally asked, staring over

warily at the **GROUCHY**, finger-munching cat.

The **GROUCHY**, finger-munching cat stared back, its one fang glinting.

Dylan shivered.

"Don't think so," I said, shaking my head. "Y'know, maybe that cat acted mean because it's been treated cruelly in the past."

"Or maybe it acted mean because it used to be a starving stray, and it thought that Fee was going to reach in and steal its food," suggested Soph.

"Or maybe it's just *plain* mean," muttered Dylan.

Maybe he was right.

Maybe someone had handed the cat

into the *Paws For Thought* Rescue Centre 'cause it spent all day lying in wait and slashing at its owner's ankles for fun.

"Well, I guess we should go and catch up with Mum and Fee," I said half-heartedly.

But none of us moved. Me, Soph and Dylan, we weren't doing very well at cheering her up, and all of us knew that we were probably the last people she wanted to see right now.

In fact, I bet she'd *rather* see one of Garfield's fleas instead of us right now.

"Seven's a lucky number."

That was Dylan.

Dylan coming out with one of those things-that-don't-make-sense. He does that a lot.

"What ARE you on about?" I asked him.

"We should *try* and think of something else to cheer Fee up before we go see her," he said, as if that made everything clear. (It didn't.)

"Well, yeah," Soph nodded, her arms crossed over her chest. "But what's that got to do with seven being a lucky number?"

"Me telling jokes, that was number **1**," Dylan started to explain, holding his fingers up as he began to reel off Cheer Up

Fee Plans. "Indie, you making cookies, that was number **2**."

"Oh, I get it. So buying the squishy cat toy was number **3**," Soph joined in. "And number **4** was when Indie was going to explain to Miss Levy about Garfield so Fee didn't have to."

Hmm. That was the **Cheer Up** Plan that nearly became the How-To-Lose-A-Friend-By-Putting-Your-Foot-In-It Plan.

"Number **5** was watching Caitlin's DVD," Dylan carried on.

"And number **6** was the Magical Mystery Tour," I mumbled, staring around at all the cages of cats, NONE of whom would be going home with Fee today.

BOO...

"So we need to think about **Cheer Up Fee** Plan No. 7," said Dylan. "And like I said, seven is a lucky number, so it's *bound* to work!"

Huh! The pot-bellied pig outside had a better chance of being asked to present the weather report on telly than we had of coming up with a plan that was *bound* to work...

"I KNOW! Why don't we all think of the one thing that cheers us up when we're sad?" Soph suddenly said. "And maybe that would work for Fee too?"

OK. That seemed like quite a cool idea.

"You go first, then, Soph," I told her, while I tried to think of a good answer.

"Um…"

Me and Dylan looked at Soph and waited patiently.

"Errr…"

Soph was nibbling at her lip and rolling her eyes up at the roof, as if a very good idea might be hiding up there.

"Hmmm…"

"I'll go first, then!" Dylan offered, when he realized we could be standing here staring at Soph all day. Or at least till someone came to lock up the cat building for the night.

"Yeah? So what makes *you* happy when you're feeling sad, Dylan?"

"Your dad offering to play PlayStation 2 with me, Indie," he said. "And me beating him."

It made me goose-pimply pleased to hear that – it was great to know that my dad could make my step-brother feel good. (It made me feel goose-pimply weird too, in that *slightly-jealous-but-not-really* way you get when you don't live with your dad and somebody else does.)

"That's nice…" I said. "But I don't think Fee will really want to play PlayStation 2 with my dad."

"Guess not," shrugged Dylan. "So what makes *you* feel better, Indie?"

I didn't think I could think of anything, when there was blast of a memory from last week.

One minute I'd been crying, and the

next minute, I'd been giggling uncontrollably.

"I was watching Newsround, and it was so SAD 'cause it was about starving children in the Sudan," I started to tell my friends. "Next thing, Dibbles wandered into the room and licked my toes till they tickled!"

Hee hee hee hee hee

Soph and Dylan were sniggering along with me, but they knew – just like I did – that Fee wouldn't really like it if we turned up with Dibbles and told her to get her shoes and socks off.

"Oh, *I* know!" Soph finally announced.

Hurray! Maybe Soph was about to come up with the perfect answer.

Or maybe not.

"When I'm miserable, my daddy picks me up and spins me till I laugh *so much* that I'm nearly SICK!"

Hee hee ha ha ha ha hee

Let me think.

If me, Dylan and Soph tried to pick Fee up and spin her around, I think she might get hysterical. And I don't mean that in a good way.

Soph's smile sank away, as she realized her suggestion hadn't come up with anything doable.

"Oh, Indie … how are we going to cheer up Fee?" she murmured sadly.

It was then that I got hit by another

(A **BLAM!** of an idea doesn't hurt, in case you were worried…)

"Wait a minute – Fee doesn't need to cheer up!"

Dylan and Soph both stared at me,

unaware of the  and reckoning that I'd gone mad.

They didn't realize that my head was full of dead goldfish.

(OK, so now anyone reading this will think I've definitely gone mad.)

"She needs to be *properly* gloomy for a while!" I announced.

Dylan and Soph kept right on staring.

"Look, when the two fin-rot goldfish died, Mum, me and Caitlin gave them a really nice, sad send-off," I tried to explain, though I guessed I sounded as muddled as Dylan sometimes did.

"What d'you mean, a nice, sad send-off?" asked Soph.

"Well, it's like a funeral."

"Yeah, but a funeral sounds *really* sad and not very nice, Indie," frowned Dylan.

"A funeral's the sad part, yes, but then you have this thing called a 'wake', that's like a happy memories party, where you eat cake and tell funny stories about whoever or whatever's died! And that's the nice part."

Me and Mum, we'd done that for the two goldfish ... buried them, planted some flowers, played sad music (thanks to Caitlin and her didgeridoo), then ate ice-cream and told funny stories about how goldfish seem to spend half their life pooing.

"So, you think we should have a 'wakey' thing for Fee?"

"For Garfield." I corrected Dylan. "Yes, 'cause I think Fee needs to be properly sad before she can be properly happy again."

So that was the start of it; not so much

Cheer Up Fee Plan No. 7
as
Let Fee Be Gloomy Plan No. 1.

And if that didn't work, then we'd just have to force Fee to play PlayStation 2, spin her round till she was sick, and let Dibbles loose on her toes...

The nice, sad
send-off

Thummma-rummmmmm-
mmmmmmm...

(That was Caitlin, or her didgeridoo, to
be more exact.)

Ssnnnifffff ... snnnnniffff...

(That was Fee, whose nose and eyes
were streaming like there was a tap somewhere in her head that couldn't be turned off.)

Hic! Hic! Hic!

(That was Dylan, who'd eaten a piece of strawberry shortcake too quickly and given himself the hiccups.)

Thudda-dudda-dudda!!

(That was Dibbles's tail, smacking happily against the ground. Like my other two dogs, he was *very* excited to be in Fee's garden, and didn't seem to realize it was supposed to be a sad occasion.)

Yep, it was Thursday afternoon, and it was officially Garfield's funeral.

When we'd caught up with Fee and Mum in the office yesterday and suggested the funeral, Fee's eyes had lit up for the first time in days.

"We'll do it properly," I'd said.

"With sad music?" Fee had asked hopefully.

"Yes, with sad music," I'd promised her.

"And could I read out the poem I wrote about G-Garfield?"

"Of course. We can have sad music and lovely poems and flowers and everything!"

Fee had smiled a wibbly smile.

"We'll all wear something black," Soph had added.

"And I'll ask my mum to make something nice to eat for the wakey!" Dylan chipped in.

Fee had looked a bit confused about the wakey bit, but her eyes had kept right on shining.

And now here we were, standing around by the side of Fee's garden shed, where her dad had buried Garfield last week.

The music was very sad: Fee had

chosen "My Heart Will Go On" from the movie *Titanic*. Caitlin didn't really know it (she likes **LOUD** rock music better), but whatever she was playing sounded good and sad anyway.

Soph had read out Fee's poem about Garfield, and how *"nice"* and *"cuddly"* he was (Fee had been too choked up to do it). Soph had her black polo-neck sleeves pulled down so you couldn't see the scratch Garfield had given her that had never quite healed.

As for flowers, Mum had cut some roses off our bush in the garden for me to take along. Fee loved their purply-pink colour, but I think Garfield would have liked their sharp thorns better.

"There…" I muttered, placing the bunch of roses on the ground, as the

thumma-rumma-rumming

didgeridoo tune came to a close.

"Bye, Garfield," whispered Fee, leaning over to gently drop a few chocolate cat treats on the ground.

Uh-oh...

"Right! Time for the wake!" I said brightly, hooking my arm into Fee's and spinning her round.

I didn't know which one of my dogs was going to get to the chocolate cat treats first, but Fee didn't need to see that.

"I'll pour the drinks," said Soph, hurrying towards the green plastic garden table and the big jug of raspberry and banana smoothie that Mrs Dean had made for us.

"The – **HIC!** – shortcake's really

ace," said Dylan, pointing to one of the three plates of goodies that Fiona had made and sent along.

The butterscotch Rice Krispie cookies looked *pretty yummy* too.

And so did the jammy cream tarts.

Mmm ... when would it be polite to get stuck in? It was hard to know, since Fee had lost her appetite.

"That was *really* lovely..." Fee sighed, sort of wistful and happy at the same time.

"Yes, it was the **BEST** cat funeral I've ever been to," said Soph, wafting the plate of strawberry shortcake under Fee's nose.

With her head lost in thoughts of the funeral, Fee didn't seem to notice that she'd helped herself to a biscuit. And

yay!

started to nibble at it.

HURRAY NO. 1:

Fee's appetite was coming back!

HURRAY NO. 2:

That meant we could all eat!!

Strawberry shortcakes, butterscotch biscuits and jammy cream tarts quickly found their way to our mouths.

"Pretty garden, Fee," said Caitlin, now that she'd put her didgeridoo to one side and come to check out the nibbles.

"Mmm," murmured Fee. "Garfield used to love it. He liked to sit on the shed and look around."

For small animals to pounce on, I thought quietly to myself.

"*And* he liked to balance his way along the back fence," said Fee, blinking hard.

Yeah, balance on the back fence before jumping into your neighbour's garden and eating his frogs, I thought again.

"And see those rhododendrons over there?"

Like I said before, Fee knows lots of big words. She's the only person in my class who would know that the huge, leafy bushes she was pointing to were called roady-wotsits.

"Yeah, I see 'em," nodded Caitlin, stuffing a whole butterscotch biscuit in her mouth and reaching for another two.

"He *loved* crawling under there. It was like his den."

More like the graveyard for bits of chewed small things, I thought, but didn't dare say.

"Cool," said Caitlin. "I'd definitely like to live here if I was a cat. So when are you going to get another one?"

urgh.

I froze.

So did Soph and Dylan.

We looked like we were playing Musical Statues, only with biscuits.

Why had Caitlin said that?

I'd told her last night about what had happened at the *Paws For Thought* Rescue Centre, with Fee getting all upset and everything.

But I'd thought at the time that Caitlin had been only been *half-listening* – she'd been too busy fishing dead fin-rot goldfish number three out of the tank at the time.

"Um, Fee doesn't WANT another cat," I reminded Caitlin hurriedly.

As soon as I said it, I had a flurry of a thought.

The one goldfish that was left, he had lacy edges and half a fin, but he was the right colour of orange to make Mum think he *wasn't* going to die like the others.

And now he needed a home, especially since he was all alone, without his fishy friends.

Maybe Fee would feel sorry enough to let her heart melt and be his new owner!

"NO," said Fee, suddenly staring hard at me.

Yikes!

Had I spoken out loud, and not in my head after all?!

"I've changed my mind, Indie," said

Fee. "Y'know, I think I do want another cat. Actually, I *definitely* want another one. Caitlin's right – this garden needs another cat or it'll just be a waste!!"

"Everything fine out there, kids?" Mrs Dean's voice drifted out of the French windows.

"Yes, Mum," said Fee, quickly stuffing the last of her strawberry shortcake into her mouth. "But I want to go to the Rescue Centre. RIGHT NOW. Is that OK?"

"Absolutely!" smiled Mrs Dean, look-ing very, very happy –

happy that Fee was happy,

happy that Fee was eating,

and happy that Fee seemed keen on getting herself a little kitty.

"Dylan, you were right – seven is a lucky number!" I whispered to him, as me and Soph started hurrying after Fee.

Cheer Up Fee Plan No. 7 was going to work after all, even if it had taken a roundabout way to happen!

Dylan blinked for a second, then broke into a cheeky smile.

"Yes, it is, isn't it?" he grinned, filling his pockets with one, two, three, four, five, six, seven yummy biscuits before follow-ing us inside…

And happy(ish) ever after!

Caitlin had taken the dogs — and the didgeridoo — home.

The rest of us were in the *Paws For Thought* Rescue Centre. (Here's a clue where exactly: **Miaow!!**)

SOPH: she was cuddling a wriggling armful of fluff (i.e. three tabby kittens).

DYLAN: he was holding out a butterscotch biscuit to an uninterested Persian cat.

ME AND MUM: we were standing by the closed door of the cat block, watching Fee stroll up and down the cages with Mrs Dean.

"I was thinking," I said softly to Mum, "that maybe Fee would like the last fin-rot goldfish too? If it definitely looks like it isn't going to die?"

"*Well*, she might have her hands full, if she's going to be taking care of a new kitten, Indie," Mum pointed out.

"Yes, but one little goldfish doesn't take a lot of looking after..."

I mean, One, Two, Three, Four and Five (and Brian the Angelfish) didn't need much more than regular food, some nice swishy fake seaweed to swim in and out of, and an occasional cleaning out.

"Well, let's just see," said Mum.

"Let's just see" … that's one of those things parents come out with instead of just saying "no".

But the way I saw it, if Fee had a new cat AND a new goldfish to look after, she definitely wouldn't have time to miss Garfield any more.

"I want ALL of these!" said Soph, walking carefully over with the cutesome threesome. "Which one do you think Fee will pick?"

"She might not pick any of them," Dylan said with a shrug, as he ambled over to join us too.

He was nibbling at the biscuit the Persian had ignored. I hoped the cat hadn't given it a trial lick first.

"What do you mean, Fee might not pick one of these?" hissed Soph, so that Fee and her mum didn't overhear. "All the kittens in this place are gorgeous, but these are the MOST gorgeous ... ist!"

If Fee had been within listening distance, she would probably have told Soph that there was no such word as gorgeous-ist, but she was too far away for that.

Dylan wasn't though.

"There's no such word as gorgeous-ist. And Fee might not choose a kitten anyway. That's what I mean."

"Dylan's right," Mum jumped in, in a small, whispering voice. "Maybe Fee will choose a full-grown cat."

"I s'pose," I nodded, thinking about all the loveable adult cats who were desperate for new homes.

Yeeeeee-AAR RRRRRRGH!!

The noise – it sounded like a Kung Fu warrior springing into action.

Instead, it was the sound of a deranged fur-demon flinging himself onto the mesh of its cage door, claws bared and one fang glistening.

A fur-demon that acted an awful lot like Garfield.

"Oh, poor puss…" cooed Fee, frowning at the growly, finger-munching cat that had taken a chunk out of her finger yesterday. "It's trying to tell us it wants out, isn't it?"

I thought it was more like it wanted to tell us that it fancied eating another chunk of Fee's finger, and *maybe* a chunk of her cheek too.

"Y'know, I think it's maybe better *not* to let it out," Mum said suddenly, zooming over to the growly cat's cage. "This one's a bit, well, *feisty*. It's bitten and scratched nearly every member of staff here."

"It won't bite me. Again, I mean," said Fee, reaching in and pulling out a startled, grouchy, finger-munching cat.

It was so startled, it let itself be draped over Fee's arm, and only growled a little bit.

(Meanwhile, me, Soph, Dylan, Mum and Mrs Dean all looked on, with fingers crossed tightly behind our backs. We were crossing them tightly, wishing that the grouchy cat wouldn't bite Fee again. And I don't know about the others, but I was also crossing my fingers and hoping that Fee didn't seriously want to take the cat home with her.)

"This is the one! I'm going to have this one. *Please*, Mrs Kidd!"

"Are you sure, Fee?" Mum asked her warily.

"Absolutely!" beamed Fee. "And I will call it Mrs Mumbles!"

She gave Mrs Mumbles a squeeze.

Mrs Mumbles hissed.

I decided instantly that if Mrs Mumbles was going to be Fee's new cat, then I wasn't going to let the fin-rot goldfish anywhere near Fee's house.

"Um, Fee – the problem is that Mrs Mumbles is actually a boy…" said Mum, frowning an apology Fee's way.

"I don't care – it's a lovely name,"

murmured Fee, as she kissed the top of Mrs Mumbles's head and got a low, mean growl in reply.

Mum looked a bit worried.

Mrs Dean looked a bit worried.

Soph and Dylan looked a bit worried.

But the good thing was that Fee looked very, very happy.

Hurray!

"Mrs Mumbles is perfect!" I told her.

It wasn't the *perfect* name, or the *perfect* cat, but it made *perfect* sense if this grouchy cat helped get Fee back to normal.

"Biscuit?" asked Dylan, staring warily at Mrs Mumbles and offering me a strawberry shortcake biscuit at the same time.

Yes, *everything* was just about perfect.

My friend was HAPPY.

My step-mum made GREAT food.

And not ALL of the fin-rot goldfish had died.

Which left one last problem.

"Mum…" I muttered.

"Yes, Indie?" said Mum, gazing down at me, with a stray piece of hay in her hair (as usual).

"Could WE maybe keep the last fin-rot goldfish?"

Mum broke into a smile.

"Well, we've got one cat, three dogs, an angelfish and five goldfish. So another tiny mouth to feed shouldn't be too hard. What shall we call it: Six?"

Mum was thinking of One, Two, Three, Four and Five, of course.

But I wasn't sure... Even though it was much better now, the new goldfish had a heap of holes in its tail and missing bits of fin. It didn't seem like a proper goldfish; maybe only a goldfish-ish. More like half a fish.

"We'll call him Five-and-a-half!" I announced, and took a big bite of my strawberry shortcake.

"One, Two, Three,

Four, Five, and Five-and-a-half?" Mum repeated, grinning broadly at me.

Y'know, after a yucky, gloomy week, I decided that if anyone asked me this second if we were having fun yet, I'd say

YES, YES, YES!!

'Cause right now, me and my friends were starting to have the best, most gorgeous-ist time, I was sure.

(Just as long as Mrs Mumbles never got her claws into Five-and-a-half…)